DC COMICS SUPER HEROES

Curious Fox
a capstone company-publishers for children

Published by Curious Fox,
an imprint of Capstone
Global Library Limited,
7 Pilgrim Street, London,
EC4V 6LB –
Registered company number: 6695582

www.curious-fox.com

ISBN 978 1 78202 354 8
20 19 18 17 16
10 9 8 7 6 5 4 3 2 1

A full catalogue for this book is available from the British
Library.

Editor: Christopher Harbo
Designer: Hilary Wacholz

Printed and bound in China.

DC COMICS™
SUPER HEROES

BATMAN™ & ROBIN™
ADVENTURES

CLAYFACE'S SLIME SPREE

BY LAURIE S. SUTTON

ILLUSTRATED BY
LUCIANO VECCHIO

BATMAN CREATED BY BOB KANE

CONTENTS

CHAPTER 1

MEET THE MASTER OF MUD

Batman swooped through the air above the dark streets of Gotham City. He used his Batrope to swing between the tall buildings. His black cape spread out behind him like a giant bat flying across the sky. His sight was as sharp as an eagle's. Batman searched for trouble. It was his job to protect the citizens of Gotham City from crime and the threat of super-villains. He was very good at it. There was only one other person who was almost as good, and that was his partner, Robin. Together, they were the Dynamic Duo.

Robin perched on the edge of a high rooftop a few blocks away from Batman. His mask helped protect his eyes from the gusty wind as he looked down at the streets below for crooks and criminals. Sure enough, he spotted a suspicious figure sneaking down an alley. Robin decided to investigate.

Robin leaped off the roof and made a swan dive towards a nearby flagpole. *SWOOSH!* He swung around the pole like an Olympic gymnast to gain speed, then let go. Robin flew over the suspect and landed in front of him.

"Don't you know it's dangerous to be out so late at night?" Robin said.

The man was so startled that he dropped the bag he was holding. Jewellery tumbled out of it. The man looked down at the gems on the ground and then up at Robin. Then he ran.

"Why do they always run?" Robin sighed. "I always catch them."

Robin picked up the dropped jewels and started after the thief. As he ran, he noticed a dark shadow pass above him. He knew it wasn't a cloud. Robin chased the crook through the alley, jumping over the trash cans that the bad guy threw in his path.

The obstacles didn't slow down Robin. He used one of them like a diving board to spring into the air. Robin tucked his body into a ball and hurtled towards the criminal. *POW!* He slammed into the fleeing felon.

"Nice work," a voice said from above.

Robin didn't have to look up to see who had spoken.

"Thanks, Batman," he replied as he snapped Bat-cuffs on the crook's wrists.

The Dark Knight slid down to the ground on a Batrope and landed next to his partner. A moment later a Gotham City police car arrived. Robin handed over the thief to the officer. Just before the Dynamic Duo resumed their nightly patrol they heard an alert come over the squad car radio.

"Attention all units! Robbery attempt in progress at WayneTech!" the dispatcher said.

Batman and Robin didn't wait. They fired their Batropes towards the rooftops and swooped towards the emergency.

WayneTech was a company owned by Batman in his other identity of billionaire businessman Bruce Wayne. It was where he secretly worked on all his special gadgets and technology.

"Do you think one of our arch-enemies is trying to steal Batman tech?" Robin asked.

"The only way to find out is to get there – fast," Batman replied.

"Okay, first one to WayneTech gets to drive the Batmobile for a week," Robin challenged his partner.

Batman nodded and instantly pulled ahead of Robin. The race was on! The Dynamic Duo leaped from rooftop to rooftop across the skyline of Gotham City. They soared through the air on Batropes and ran through the alleys between buildings. Suddenly Robin lost sight of the Dark Knight.

"Uh-oh. He probably found a shortcut," Robin said and increased his speed.

Batman's shortcut was fast, but not very pleasant. He ran through the underground storm drain system. It was mucky and damp, but it was as straight as a ruler and led directly to the WayneTech building.

The Dark Knight burst up out of a storm grate and into chaos. The street outside of WayneTech was clogged with police cars, fire trucks and TV news vehicles. Emergency lights flashed red and blue like lightning. Batman studied the scene for a moment to analyze his surroundings and plan his strategy. A moment after that Robin dropped down from a Batrope and landed next to his partner.

"This is a lot of Emergency Response for a simple robbery attempt, even if it *is* WayneTech," Robin said.

"That depends on who the robber is," Batman replied. "Let's find out."

The Dynamic Duo avoided the flashing police lights and TV cameras. They headed for the shadows. Batman led them to a secret door into WayneTech.

Batman had designed the hidden entrance long ago just in case of an emergency like this one. All he had to do was press a button on his Utility Belt and the door opened.

Batman and Robin slipped silently into WayneTech and immediately saw a trail of destruction. Walls were smashed and security guards were slumped unconscious on the floor. Broken fire sprinklers sprayed water all over the hallway. A thin trail of brown mud swirled at the Dynamic Duo's feet. Batman swished his finger through the mud and studied it carefully. Robin leaned in to look at it, too. His eyes went wide behind his mask.

"Is that what I think it is?" Robin asked.

"Yes. It's trouble. Big trouble," the Dark Knight replied.

"Then what are we waiting for?" Robin said and rushed forward.

The Dynamic Duo followed the mud trail to a huge hole in the wall. The thick steel security door that used to be there now lay crumpled on the floor. A sign on the door identified it as Research & Development Lab #5. They heard loud voices shouting inside the room.

"Grab everything! I don't know what this stuff is, but it's WayneTech and it's worth money!" someone ordered.

"Don't point that at me! You don't know what it..." *ZAAAAP!*

"Owww!" another voice complained. "Don't test them here! Just stuff them in your bags."

Batman and Robin burst into the room. It took the Dark Knight only a few seconds to observe and evaluate the threat he and Robin faced.

The huge villain looked like a big blob of clay, but he wasn't anything like a child's mud pie. He was stealing experimental technology with the help of his henchmen. They grabbed things off of shelves and lab tables and put them into bags. The super-villain grabbed gadgets and stuffed them inside his shifting body made of mud.

"Clayface!" Batman said.

The brown blob who was once a man twisted to face the Dark Knight.

Clayface laughed. "I guess it's slime time, Batman," he said and shot oozing tendrils from his body towards the crime fighter.

Batman dodged the muddy assault. Clayface missed his enemy and hit his own minions instead. *SPLOOSH!* They suffered the fate meant for the Dark Knight.

Clayface pulled the tendrils back into his body with a slurping sound. Robin pounced on the stunned helpers and wrapped them up in a net.

"That sure made my job easy. Thanks, Clayface!" Robin said as he sat on top of the pile of captured henchmen.

The gooey villain roared his frustration and used his shape-shifting powers to form a huge hammer arm to break through the wall. *BWAAAM!* He fled through the opening and the Dynamic Duo followed him into a garage filled with experimental vehicles.

"Wow!" Robin gasped. "These cars are great!"

"Yes, but they have major flaws, too," Batman warned. "We can't let Clayface get away with any of them."

VROOM! SCREECH!

Suddenly a vehicle zoomed towards the Dynamic Duo. Clayface was at the steering wheel. The experimental car sprouted wings, then it deployed boat propellers. The tyres retracted and were replaced by ski skids. Sparks flew everywhere! Then everything reversed and the vehicle was a car again.

"It looks like Clayface has found a car with multi-morphing controls," Batman said.

"Ha! I like this car. Its shape changes just like I do!" Clayface said.

The super-villain accelerated towards the Dynamic Duo. Batman pushed Robin out of harm's way and stood like a guardian between Clayface and escape. Then he pulled a Batarang from his Utility Belt.

"Is that all you've got?" Clayface taunted. He pressed a random control and a slick spray of oil shot out at the Dark Knight.

Batman dodged the threat and threw the Batarang. It hit the hood of the vehicle and stuck there.

Nothing happened.

Clayface zoomed past the Dark Knight, crashed through the garage wall, and careened into the street. The prototype vehicle shimmered and became invisible.

"I see he found the stealth mode," Batman said.

A parked news van was thrown onto its side and a police car was shoved onto the pavement as Clayface struggled with the cloaked car's steering controls.

"He's getting away!" Robin complained.

"Don't worry, Robin," Batman said. "Remember what I taught you: they always run, but we always catch them."

CHAPTER 2

FIGHTING DIRTY

Batman didn't head off after Clayface right away. He surprised Robin by walking back into the lab. The Dark Knight went around the room and picked up a selection of odd-looking devices.

"Grab that sonic scrambler," Batman said to Robin and pointed at a small black sphere. "We might need the micro air cannon, too."

"What are these things?" Robin asked.

"They're prototypes," Batman explained. "WayneTech is developing them for, well, let's just say they are for crime prevention."

Robin understood. The gadgets were inventions secretly meant for Batman.

"But be careful, everything is highly experimental and hasn't been field-tested yet," Batman warned. "There's a chance that nothing will work, or that something will fail in the middle of operation."

"Sounds like fun," Robin said and rolled what looked like a tangled ball of yarn around in his hands. He was about to throw it in the air when the Dark Knight cautioned his partner to stop.

"That's a multi-volt constricting snare," Batman said. He pointed at a small rod inside the twist of fibres. "It will deliver quite a jolt of electricity."

"Then I'll save it for Clayface," Robin said. "Let's go and get him!"

The Dynamic Duo slipped out of the lab just as the police and firefighters arrived. Police Commissioner Gordon and his officers found Clayface's captured henchmen all wrapped up and waiting to be arrested. Gordon caught a glimpse of Batman's cape fluttering through the hole in the lab wall and knew who had caught the bad guys.

"He makes my job easy," Gordon said.

While the authorities mopped up the mess in the rest of the WayneTech building, Batman and Robin returned to the garage that held the experimental vehicles.

"We need to catch up with Clayface, and fast," the Dark Knight declared. "It looks like a couple of these prototypes are going to get field-tested ahead of schedule."

"All right!" Robin said. He raced towards what looked like a sports car and popped opened the driver's side door.

"Not so fast," Batman said to his partner. "Remember what I said about the prototypes having major flaws? The emergency ejector seat on that car is unreliable."

"That doesn't sound like the kind of ride I need tonight," Robin said. Then he ran over to another vehicle parked near by. It resembled a one-person armoured car.

"How about this one?" Robin asked hopefully.

Batman shook his head no. Robin's shoulders slumped and he looked down at the floor with dramatic disappointment. The Dark Knight walked over to a pair of sleek motorcycles. They looked like black torpedoes on wheels.

"Let me introduce you to the ultra-turbo 'Stinger' cycle," Batman said. "Zero-to-max in 30 seconds, enhanced radar and sonar, and..."

Batman touched a button. Bat-shaped wings deployed.

"Yes!" Robin said with a fist pump.

The Dynamic Duo jumped onto the two prototype motorcycles. They revved their engines and zoomed through the hole in the garage made by Clayface.

As they rode through the streets of Gotham City in pursuit of the muddy menace, they could see where Clayface had been. He had left a trail of dented cars and frightened pedestrians.

"Wow. Clayface sure is a lousy driver," Robin said.

"The steering system on that prototype hasn't been perfected. The vehicle is hard to control," Batman replied. He spoke to Robin through a radio that linked the two bikes. "I just hope Clayface doesn't hurt anyone before we can catch up with him."

Even though the villain had an invisible car, the Batarang stuck on its hood had a locator device. The Dynamic Duo followed the signal.

"Hmmm ... even when the vehicle is in stealth mode I can receive a tracking signal," Batman said. "I'll have to fix that in the next design phase. But right now it works in our favour."

The Dynamic Duo followed the tracking signal towards a crossroads not far away. From a distance, they could hear drivers honking their car horns impatiently.

When Batman and Robin arrived on the scene, they saw that the stolen experimental vehicle was stalled in the middle of the crossroads. A traffic jam surrounded the broken-down prototype.

The operator of a late-night bus blew its horn. *HONK! HONK!* The noise annoyed Clayface. He oozed out of the experimental vehicle and waved multiple gooey limbs at the bus driver. The man was startled at first, but then he got angry.

"Hey! Get outta the way! I've got a timetable! Yer makin' me late!" the bus driver shouted.

Clayface formed giant hammer arms and clubbed the front of the bus. The vehicle bounced on its tyres and all of its windows shattered. The passengers shrieked in alarm.

"You're out of service," Clayface declared.

Batman and Robin zoomed up on their motorcycles, and the Dark Knight launched himself at the man of mud. Batman's boots met Clayface, up close and personal. *SQUOOOSH!!* He sank in up to his knees.

Clayface stumbled backwards from the blow. While the villain was off balance, Robin moved in. He leaped straight at Clayface and pushed the experimental sonic scrambler into the villain's muddy mass. *SHREEEEEE!* A high-pitched sound struck Robin's ears. All the glass windows and light fixtures around them shattered. The pavement under their feet started to crack.

Clayface began to vibrate from the sound waves. His gooey body rippled and started to lose its shape. Batman pulled free from the mucky mass. He rolled away from the super-villain and got back to his feet.

"The sonic scrambler is working. It's scrambling Clayface. Cool!" Robin said.

Suddenly the shrill sound stopped. Clayface's mass returned to its normal composition.

"Uh-oh. I guess the sonic scrambler is a dud," Robin said as he shrugged.

Clayface opened his mouth and shot clay cannonballs at the young crime fighter. Robin dodged the goo balls. He leaped onto the top of a car and then to the strut of a tall street lamp. He twisted and twirled like a circus acrobat. Robin built up speed and then let go of the strut. He smashed into Clayface the same way Batman had done earlier.

Robin sank into Clayface's goopy mass up to his knees too. But he wasn't worried. It was part of his plan.

"Let's see how well this micro air cannon works," Robin said.

Robin took the WayneTech device and shoved it into the villain's shifting body. The micro air cannon looked and worked just like its description. Robin pulled a trigger and a blast of compressed air shot into Clayface. The villain expanded like a balloon!

"What ... what's happening to me?" Clayface yelled. His arms and legs stuck out from his giant round body. His head looked like a ping-pong ball on top of a basketball. In a few seconds he was too awkward to stand up. Clayface tipped over onto his face.

"Bluuurrf! Muuuurf!" Clayface mumbled helplessly.

Robin pulled himself free from the villain's gooey body.

Robin kicked the inflated super-villain like a football. Clayface bounced off the side of the bus he'd wrecked and over the tops of the stalled cars. Batman leaped into the air and delivered a backwards kick. Clayface bounced back towards Robin.

"He shoots, he scores!" Robin said as he kicked for a goal. The super-round super-villain got wedged between a parking sign and a lamppost.

"I'll get you for this," Clayface said in a squeaky voice. His face was squished on both sides.

"The only thing you're getting is jail time," Batman replied.

Robin held the micro air cannon out in front of him and grinned. The device dripped with muddy drops from Clayface's mucky mass.

"Hey, this prototype actually worked. I guess it passes the field test," Robin said.

Clayface did not stay inflated for long. He opened his mouth and expelled the air from his body with a loud belch. Clayface returned to his normal size. He wiggled out from between the lamppost and parking sign and shot thick ribbons of muck towards Batman and Robin. *SPLAT!*

The muck knocked Robin into the side of the bus. He slumped to the street. Batman pulled a Batarang from his Utility Belt and threw it at Clayface. The villain simply absorbed it into his mucky mass. He wasn't afraid of a plain old Batarang, but he should have been. *ZZZWAAAAP!* Clayface shook from head to toe. The stolen WayneTech devices vibrated out of the super-villain's body and dropped to the ground.

"Ohhhh, what hit me?" Clayface mumbled as he quivered.

"I attached the experimental multi-volt constricting snare to an ordinary Batarang," Batman replied. "It seems that this device has passed the field test, too."

Suddenly a fountain of mud rose up out of Clayface. Bobbing at the top of it was the Batarang with the multi-volt device still attached. Clayface commanded the fountain to throw the device at the Dark Knight. As the electrified snare flew towards Batman, Robin threw a Batarang. *KZIIING!* It knocked the device to the ground where it sputtered, sparked and shorted out.

"These prototypes are the pits," Robin declared.

"Then it's time to go back to good, old-fashioned low tech," Batman said.

The Dark Knight pulled a grapnel from his Utility Belt and launched it at Clayface. The villain let it hit his gooey body and sink into his mass. Robin followed Batman's example and fired a second grapnel into the criminal. Clayface laughed at their efforts.

"A couple of Batropes aren't going to stop me," Clayface said.

"It's not the Batropes you should be worried about," Robin replied.

"Wait for it," Batman told Clayface.

Suddenly Clayface felt his insides heat up. His body started to become hard and brittle.

"There were flares attached to the Batropes," Batman said to the surprised super-villain. "Their extreme heat is baking your clay into pottery."

Clayface gulped. "Uh-oh," he said.

CHAPTER 3

SLIME IN THE STREETS

Batman and Robin watched the sludgy super-villain start to solidify. Clayface tried to expel the flares from his body, but they had already done their work. His torso was as solid as stone.

"Now that's what I call a hardened criminal," Robin said.

"Indeed," Batman replied. "But be on your guard, Robin, this muddy menace is full of tricks."

Batman was right. Clayface couldn't move the middle of his body, but he could reshape his head, arms and legs. He turned what he had left of his gooey form into slick slime and slid it under the solidified part of him. He looked like a freaky snail as he tried to ooze away from the Dynamic Duo.

"Not so fast," Batman said.

The Dark Knight launched a micro-mesh net over Clayface and sealed it up like a big bag. The metallic weave was so tight that even Clayface had difficultly passing through it. The super-villain struggled inside the net.

"It looks like you've netted a big one, Batman," Robin said.

Suddenly a thin, brown liquid started dripping from the micro-mesh. The drops hit the ground and formed a puddle at Batman's feet. The puddle moved as if it were alive.

"I think the big one is trying to get away," Batman said.

A face formed in the puddle.

"You costumed do-gooders always underestimate me," Clayface declared. "I can ooze through the smallest opening."

The puddle thickened and turned into the mucky villain. He re-formed and confronted the Dynamic Duo.

"You can't contain me!" Clayface proclaimed victoriously.

"That's not completely true," Batman corrected. He shook the micro-mesh net. "The part of you that's baked solid can't get out. You're not whole without it."

The shocked look on Clayface's face revealed that he hadn't thought about that.

"You're only half the super-villain you used to be," Robin said.

"Arrrrgh!" Clayface roared and tried to grab the net from Batman.

Clayface shot a thick tendril of goo towards the Dark Knight, but Batman was ready for an attack. He dodged the assault and threw the bundled net to Robin. Clayface pulled his tendril back into his body and turned his attention to Batman's junior partner.

Robin caught the bag and launched a grapnel. It grabbed onto the ledge of a nearby building. Robin retracted the Batrope attached to it and was pulled up to the rooftop. Clayface turned his whole body into a fountain of liquid mud and shot up towards Robin on the roof.

SLOOSH!

When Clayface got to the top of the building he looked around for his young foe. What he saw made him furious. Robin stood on the ledge of the building and threw the mesh net back to Batman on the street below.

"Noooo!" Clayface yelled.

Robin waved goodbye to Clayface and swooped away on his Batrope. Clayface rushed to the ledge and watched the two costumed crime fighters congratulate each other. Batman looked up at Clayface. He dropped the net onto the street and calmly crossed his arms. The sight infuriated Clayface. He hurtled down from the roof at an angry pace. That was just what Batman had planned.

"Heads up, Robin," Batman said. "He's not thinking straight, and that makes him extra dangerous."

"Got it. But if he's mad now, he's *really* going to hate Operation Hot Potato," Robin replied with a grin.

Clayface raced towards the Dynamic Duo. He was as mad as a charging rhino, and his shape-shifting body took on that form. Clayface galloped on four thick legs and lowered double horns at his two enemies.

"Grrronk!" Clayface bellowed.

Batman threw the mesh net to Robin and ran straight at the threat. He twirled a Batrope like a lasso above his head as he ran. Clayface's thoughts were so clouded by anger that he didn't understand what the Dark Knight was about to do.

Batman looped the Batrope around Clayface's rhino horns and dug in his heels like a champion cattle roper.

FLIP! WHOMP!

Rhino Clayface went down. He skidded down the street and crashed into the wrecked bus. The crowd on the street cheered Batman and booed Clayface.

"Yay! Get him, Batman!"

"The bigger they are, the harder they fall!"

"Booo! Clayface is all wet!"

"You're going down the drain, Clayface!"

The super-villain felt dazed by the blow. He wasn't used to that. He wasn't used to being separated from a large portion of his muddy mass, either. He wasn't whole. He had to retrieve the part of him that was in the mesh net. He had to get it back from Batman and Robin!

Clayface oozed out from the coils of the Batrope. He looked around for Robin and the mesh net. A shout from above drew his attention to the top of a statue. Clayface saw Robin waving at him from the rump of a bronze horse. Clayface roared in anger and shot towards the monument. *SPLOOSH!* He covered the statue from hoof to tail.

"I've got you now," Clayface said.

"No, you don't," Robin replied from the window-sill of a nearby building.

"What? How did you...?" Clayface gasped.

Robin zoomed higher up the side of the building on his Batrope.

"You're almost as slippery as me," Clayface said. He turned himself into a geyser and gushed upwards at his foe.

Just before Clayface reached Robin, Batman swooped between them and took the mesh net from his partner. Suddenly Robin wasn't weighed down with the solidified mass of Clayface anymore. He was able to zip upwards with extra speed. Clayface missed Robin and hit the side of the building instead. *SMOOSH!* Batman watched the gooey super-villain slide down the surface of the building.

"He's finished," Robin said as he landed on the rooftop next to his partner.

"I'm going to make sure. Hold onto this and stay here. No matter what," Batman said as he handed the bundled net to Robin.

The Dark Knight slid down his Batrope to the street. The puddle of goo that was Clayface didn't move. A crowd of onlookers formed around the fallen super-villain.

"Is ... is he dead?" someone asked.

"No. He's just stunned," Batman replied. He made a sweeping motion with his hands and cape. "Everyone get away. It's not safe."

The crowd did as Batman asked, except one man – the bus driver.

"This super-creep wrecked my bus!" the driver shouted. He stomped his foot into the ooze.

Suddenly the ooze climbed up the driver's leg. It spread in a thin layer over his whole body in only a few seconds. Everything was covered except his nose and mouth.

A face formed in the goo on the driver's chest. Clayface was awake!

"Stand back, Batman!" Clayface warned. "Or this bus driver gets a mouthful of mud."

"Help!" the bus driver yelped.

"Let him go, Clayface," Batman said.

"I'll let him go if you give me that net," Clayface said.

Batman looked up at Robin on the rooftop above them. Robin held the mesh net.

"No," Batman replied.

"What?!" Clayface and the bus driver shouted at the same time.

Batman reached into his Utility Belt. He pulled out a small cylinder.

"This is a capsule of liquid nitrogen," Batman said. "It will freeze *anything* on contact. I used high heat on you, Clayface. Do you want to try extreme cold?"

"If you freeze me, you freeze the bus driver," Clayface said.

"No, I won't. As long as you're covering him, you're insulating him. You're like a big blanket," Batman told Clayface.

"Do it, Batman," the bus driver said. "I trust you."

Clayface's expression on the driver's chest looked worried.

"Surrender, Clayface," Batman declared.

"Okay," Clayface said quietly.

Batman waited. He held the freeze capsule ready to use. He did not trust Clayface.

"Okay," Clayface repeated. "Do it. Go ahead and freeze me."

Batman was suspicious of his enemy giving up without a fight. But his suspicions didn't stop him from acting. The Dark Knight threw the freeze capsule at his foe.

Clayface looked surprised. He had been sure that Batman was bluffing. *FWOOSH!* The capsule erupted into a cloud of stinging, cold vapour in front of the villain. The close call alarmed Clayface so much that he abandoned the bus driver and slimed towards a storm drain. Along the way he grabbed one small WayneTech device that had fallen to the ground. Then he slithered through the wide grate and disappeared.

"We haven't seen the last of Clayface," Batman told Robin.

"Nope. He'll be back for this," Robin replied and shook the mesh net.

"We can use that to our advantage," Batman said. "I have a plan."

When the Gotham City police arrived they brought along a steel barrel. Batman had requested it.

"This is an odd request, Batman, even for you," Commissioner Gordon said. "What do you need it for?"

Batman opened the mesh net to show the commissioner the contents. Gordon looked shocked.

"What ... what is that?" Gordon asked as he took a step backwards.

"Clayface, or at least a part of him," the Dark Knight replied as he put the net in the barrel and welded the top shut. "He won't stay solid for very long. He'll turn back to clay soon. We need to put this barrel somewhere secure."

"I can take it to police headquarters and put it in the evidence vault," Gordon said.

"Good. That should hold him until I can capture the rest of him," Batman replied.

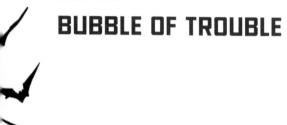

CHAPTER 4

BUBBLE OF TROUBLE

Batman and Robin sat in front of the giant monitor screen of the Batcomputer in the Batcave. They sifted through terabytes of information trying to trace the exact location of the experimental devices stolen from WayneTech. Batman knew if he could track down the stolen items he could find the thief who stole them – Clayface!

"I think the trail has gone cold, Batman. It's been two days and we haven't found even a hint of that mucky menace," Robin said.

"He hasn't left Gotham City, if that's what you're worried about," Batman assured his young partner.

"That's true. He won't go anywhere without that chunk of him we captured," Robin said. "It's a good thing that it's locked securely in the vault at police headquarters."

"All we have to do now is find and arrest the rest of him," Batman said.

A large red dot suddenly appeared on the big computer screen. A pop-up window supplied information reporting the event.

ROBBERY IN PROGRESS

GOTHAM FIRST NATIONAL BANK

500 EAST ELM ST., BETWEEN BROADWAY AND OLIVE AVE.

INCIDENT WARNINGS: PEOPLE FLOATING IN THE AIR REPORTED

"People floating in the air?" Robin said.

"That sounds like one of the experimental antigravity devices WayneTech developed," Batman declared.

"That means we've just found Clayface," Robin replied.

The Dynamic Duo jumped into the Batmobile. Batman revved the engine and released the brake. The sound of high-stress, multiple layer polymer tyres getting a grip echoed from the Batcave walls. The automatic seat safety harnesses clamped down over both occupants seconds before the Batmobile shot forward like a rocket. Batman and Robin were pressed back into their seats.

"I love this part!" Robin said. "Are you sure you won't let me drive?"

"I'm sure," Batman replied.

The Batmobile hurtled down a tunnel and out of a secret door in the side of the hill below Wayne Manor. The vehicle zoomed out of the opening and onto a roadway designed to look like natural grass and wild flowers. The vehicle flattened the artificial turf and flowers, but they bounced back up to disguise any traces of tyre tracks.

"I'm plotting the shortest route to the bank robbery at 500 East Elm Street," Robin said as he entered coordinates into the Batmobile's computer. "Initializing Gotham City traffic signals to assist."

The sleek vehicle zoomed through the streets of Gotham City. Every traffic signal turned to green as the Batmobile approached. The Dark Knight skillfully drove around cars and buses. He avoided every obstacle as if he had the senses of a bat.

Batman and Robin arrived at the Gotham First National Bank and were amazed at what they saw. People really were floating in the air! They yelled for help and churned their arms and legs as if swimming in an invisible pool. They tumbled head over heels in slow motion.

Everything inside the bubble of zero gravity floated in the air too. Trash and litter drifted randomly. Mobile phones, briefcases, handbags and hats all wafted aimlessly. Even pigeons were flapping furiously and going nowhere. A ring of police officers stood outside the sphere of weightlessness to keep onlookers from getting too close.

The Batmobile skidded to a halt in front of the bank and the Dynamic Duo leaped out to investigate. Just as they suspected, Clayface was causing all the confusion.

He stood at the top of the marble steps leading up to the bank while weightless bystanders and bank customers drifted around him. He held a bag of loot in one hand and a small device in the other hand.

"He's got a WayneTech antigravity prototype," Batman whispered to Robin. "Luckily, it generates only a small field."

"How can we turn it off?" Robin asked.

"That was part of the problem during testing," Batman admitted. "The good news is, the device has a limited power supply."

"And the bad news?" Robin asked.

"The power supply pack usually blew up," Batman replied.

"How long do you think we have until that happens?" Robin said. "All these people are in danger!"

"We can't know that for certain. It depends on when Clayface activated the device and how much energy the field is demanding from the power pack," Batman said. "I estimate we have only a few minutes to rescue everyone and capture Clayface."

"Oh, no pressure," Robin said. "What's our plan of attack?"

"First, no capes," Batman said and pulled off the long, flowing portion of his uniform.

"Huh?" Robin replied, confused.

"Have you ever seen astronauts with long hair in zero gravity?" Batman asked.

"Yes. Their hair sticks out all over the place. Ohhh! Our capes will do the same thing," Robin said.

"Yes. Capes can be a hindrance in zero gravity," Batman said.

"I'm ready!" Robin declared as he removed his colourful cape.

"Good. Operation Acrobat is about to begin ... now!" Batman said. He and Robin jumped into the antigravity field head first.

At first the Dynamic Duo floated just like everyone else inside the bubble of weightlessness. But Batman and Robin had something no one else had – their amazing acrobatic skills. Batman held his muscles perfectly still. Robin did the same thing. They found a balance point. Batman knew that every action they made would create an equal and opposite reaction. Actually, he was depending on that fact.

"Batman! Robin! The two of you can't stop me!" Clayface boasted when he saw the Dynamic Duo.

"You're wrong," Batman replied.

Batman saw that Clayface was anchored to the ground. The super-villain had wrapped gooey tendrils around the security posts in front of the bank building. Everyone except Clayface floated at random. This was exactly what the Dark Knight wanted. Clayface was stationary. But Batman was free to move!

"Operation Acrobat!" Batman told Robin.

The Dynamic Duo moved in perfect harmony. First, they grabbed each other's forearms. This gave them a shared centre of balance. Next, they touched the soles of their feet together. This gave them a launching platform. Batman and Robin pushed away from each other as hard as they could. They floated gently in opposite directions.

Clayface laughed. "Ha ha! The antigravity field makes you as slow as snails," he said to his foes.

The slimy villain stopped laughing as Batman grabbed onto one of the memorial statues in front of the bank. It gave the Dark Knight an anchor to make his next move. He pulled a grapnel from his Utility Belt. He used the powerful launcher to propel himself away from the solid stone base towards Clayface. He didn't move like a snail now.

"Uh-oh," Clayface said. He shifted his eyes towards where he had last seen Robin. The young crime fighter had copied Batman's move and was coming straight at Clayface from the other side.

Batman and Robin hit Clayface at the same time. Their feet and legs sank into him, like before, but this time the impact made parts of Clayface break into blobs. The zero gravity caused the bits to separate and float away like giant drops of water.

Clayface reached out with gooey tendrils to recapture the floating blobs. But there were too many and he couldn't catch them all. The Dynamic Duo didn't have that problem. They somersaulted though the air. They gathered up the floating pieces and sealed them in special canisters from their Utility Belts. Clayface howled in anger.

"We'll take you to jail bit by bit if we have to," Batman told his foe. "Make it easy on yourself and surrender in one piece."

"I'll never surrender!" Clayface declared, even though he was reduced to only a third of his normal size.

Suddenly steam rose up from the portion of Clayface that held the antigravity device. The prototype glowed like a hot coal.

"Ow!" Clayface yelped and released the device. It floated gently away in mid-air.

"That prototype is going to explode," Batman warned.

"Bye!" Clayface replied.

The super-villain stuffed the bag of stolen loot into his body and oozed down the steps of the bank. He used tiny tendrils to grip the grooves in the pavement and pull himself along inside the sphere of weightlessness. He looked like a mutant centipede.

Clayface passed through the barrier of the antigravity field and slimed into a storm drain. The bag of loot didn't fit through the grate. It popped out of Clayface's body and was left behind.

Batman wasn't worried about Clayface escaping. He was worried about the WayneTech prototype exploding! Everyone inside the antigravity sphere was in danger. He had to act quickly.

"Robin, Operation Fireworks!" Batman ordered.

The Dark Knight launched a powerful grapnel straight up into the air. It pierced the wall of the antigravity sphere. Then it split into smaller hooks and grapnels. They spread out like the burst of a fireworks display. Some of the mini-grapnels grabbed onto buildings and street lamps. Others dropped to the ground.

The Dark Knight didn't wait to be sure which lines were secure. He grabbed the antigravity device and zoomed upwards on the Batrope attached to the main grapnel. As he shot into the sky above the bank, the antigravity sphere went with him!

CHAPTER 5

PICKING UP THE PIECES

Batman held onto the WayneTech antigravity device and zoomed upwards on his Batrope. The bubble of weightlessness rose with him and the device.

At first everybody else inside the field still floated like feathers. They didn't move, but the antigravity bubble did. Suddenly the wall of the bubble came up under them – and they passed right through it! It was just like what had happened with Clayface and the Bat-grapnel. They broke through the barrier and Earth's normal gravity took over again.

Robin, the bank customers and the bystanders dropped to the pavement.

"Ow!"

"Oof!"

"Eek!"

Everything dropped out except the tiny pieces of litter and trash.

Batman reached the top end of the Batrope and hung in the air above the bank. He felt the device heating up in his grasp. The power pack was about to reach its limit. It was going to explode soon!

"Batman! Let me help!" Robin shouted.

Batman saw that his partner was standing on the landing skid of a police helicopter. Then he realized that there was a whole squad of police choppers swarming around the antigravity bubble.

"Let *all* of us help!" Commissioner Gordon said as he leaned out from the cockpit of another helicopter.

The WayneTech device started to sizzle through Batman's glove. He knew that anyone near the explosion might be hurt.

"I'm going to need your helicopter, Commissioner," the Dark Knight announced.

Batman launched the last grapnel from his Utility Belt. It attached to the landing gear of the chopper. He pressed a control on his Utility Belt and all the smaller "fireworks" grapnels released their grip on the surrounding buildings and street lamps. Batman didn't let go of the WayneTech device as he hung from the Batrope attached to the police chopper.

"I'm tethered to this aircraft now, and so is the antigravity device," Batman warned. "You should evacuate to another chopper."

"I'm staying!" Gordon and the pilot said together.

"Then take us higher!" Batman ordered.

The chopper pilot pulled back on the control stick and the helicopter zoomed straight up into the sky! Batman and the antigravity sphere were pulled along with it like a balloon on a string.

The skyline of Gotham City got smaller as the helicopter flew higher. Batman tied the end of the Batrope around the antigravity device and then dragged himself along the rope. Inside the sphere of weightlessness there was no "up" or "down." The only direction was where the Batrope led him.

Batman headed for the shimmering barrier wall of the antigravity bubble. He could see Commissioner Gordon reaching out for him on the other side.

The Dark Knight stretched out an arm to Gordon, but they were too far apart.

"It doesn't look like I'm going to make it out of here," Batman said. "But that doesn't mean I'm going to give up."

The Dark Knight gripped the Batrope and twisted his body. He thrust his feet up over his head. Now he had the whole length of his body to reach the edge of the antigravity field. Suddenly his boots broke through the barrier. Commissioner Gordon grabbed Batman's feet and started to pull with all his strength.

Batman popped out of the antigravity bubble. Commissioner Gordon held the Dark Knight upside down by his knees as the police chopper zoomed higher and higher. The defective WayneTech device glowed like lava not far below the helicopter.

Even though he was hanging upside down from a rapidly ascending aircraft, Batman was calm. He reached over and unfastened the grapnel from the helicopter's landing strut. The tether to the antigravity bubble was released.

"Keep climbing!" Batman said to the pilot. "Go as fast as this bird can fly!"

The chopper pilot pushed the aircraft until all the cockpit alarms and warning lights went off. Its engines whined beyond their limits. The sudden lift made Commissioner Gordon fall out of the chopper! Batman hooked his arm around his friend and wrapped his legs around the landing struts. The two men dangled dangerously. They stared down at a blinding light as the power pack on the WayneTech device blew up.

BWOOOOMMMM!

The force of the blast shook every rivet on the police chopper. The concussive wave threw Batman against the side of the chopper, but he didn't let go of Gordon. The Dark Knight used the powerful blow to help him shove the commissioner back into the cockpit. *CLICK!* Batman snapped the seat belt around the commissioner.

"Safety first," Batman reminded his friend.

"Is the city safe?" Gordon asked.

"Yes. The explosion happened very high above Gotham City. No one was hurt," the Dark Knight replied. "But there is some fall out."

Gordon and Batman watched the fall out from the sky-high explosion. All the people and animals had escaped the antigravity bubble, but not the trash and litter. A rain of rubbish fell down onto the streets!

"I'd better call the Sanitation Department to clean up this mess," Gordon said as he reached for his mobile phone.

"Good. You can clean up the streets one way, and I'll clean up the streets another way," Batman replied. "Clayface may have started this slime spree, but I'm going to finish it."

* * *

Batman and Robin watched Gotham City Police officers carry sealed barrels into a vault at police headquarters. These were very special barrels. This was a very special vault.

"These containers hold all the pieces of Clayface that have been captured so far," Commissioner Gordon told his men. "This is the safest place for them until we catch the rest of that muddy madman."

Gordon watched the officers put the barrels inside the vault. He checked all the seals on the containers and followed the officers out of the vault. The commissioner helped two officers close the thick steel door. *CLAANG!* Then he activated the security code on the electronic lock.

"Jensen and Abbey, stand guard," Gordon said to a couple of officers.

"Yes, sir!" the officers replied. They took up positions on either side of the vault.

"Clayface will never get in there," Batman said.

"He won't dare to come near police headquarters," Robin stated.

"Even if he's bold enough to try, there's no way he can get past the vault's security," Gordon said.

Batman, Robin and Commissioner Gordon walked down the corridor and out of sight. Moments later Gordon came back down the corridor. He stood in front of the two guards and smiled.

"I, um, left my phone inside the vault," Gordon said, embarrassed. "Open it up."

"We can't do that," Jensen said.

"I just gave you an order," Gordon growled.

"But, sir, you're the only one who knows the security code," Abbey explained.

"You're not going to make this easy for me, are you?" Gordon said as he changed shape. His body turned from human to mud.

"Clayface!" the officers shouted just before the super-villain knocked them out with two giant-size hammer fists.

The guards collapsed and Clayface slithered over them to the vault door. He thinned out his slime and searched for the smallest crack in the door. He sent out tiny tendrils from all over his body and ran them along the surface of the thick steel. At last he found a tiny crack and oozed through.

"So much for the vault's security," Clayface scoffed.

The slimy super-villain entered the vault. It was very chilly inside. Clayface re-formed into his normal shape, but he knew that he was not normal. Most of his mass was separated from him and sealed in barrels. He had to get it back.

Clayface looked around the vault. There were boxes and bags of police evidence. Bundles of cash seized from crime scenes and stolen property crowded the evidence vault.

Clayface knew a thief could get rich robbing the place. But he wasn't interested in any of those things. He wanted to find the barrels that held his fragments.

Suddenly the gleam of several large canisters attracted his attention. Clayface lumbered over to them. His legs felt stiff, but he ignored it. He was excited to finally free his captured pieces.

Clayface formed huge hammer hands. *BWAAANG!* He hit the barrels as hard as he could. *SKIIISH!* His hammer hands shattered! Too late, Clayface finally realized what was happening.

"It's really cold in here," Clayface said. He remembered his narrow escape from the Dark Knight's liquid nitrogen capsule.

"It's *freezing* cold," Batman corrected. "This isn't a police vault. It's a cryogenic chamber."

Batman and Robin confronted Clayface inside the chamber. They wore thermal capes to protect them from the cold. Clayface felt the freeze.

"Your trap can't contain me!" Clayface declared. He lumbered towards the Dynamic Duo. Batman and Robin didn't even flinch. The muddy menace slowed, then he froze right in front of them. Robin tapped the solidified nose of their enemy. A chunk fell off before the rest of the massive menace shattered into pieces.

Suddenly the cryogenic chamber opened. A clean-up crew from S.T.A.R. Labs entered and swept up the shards of the super-villain. The pieces were placed in a large container and the lid was sealed.

"It looks like Clayface *can* be contained after all," Batman said.

CLAYFACE

REAL NAME: Matt Hagen

OCCUPATION: Professional criminal

BASE: Gotham City

ABILITIES: Shapeshifting, impressionist, professional actor

HEIGHT: Varies

WEIGHT: Varies

EYES: Varies

HAIR: None

Formerly a big name in the film industry, actor Matt Hagen had his face, and career, ruined in a tragic car crash. Hoping to regain his good looks, Hagan accepted the help of ruthless businessman Roland Daggett, who gave him a special cream that allowed Hagen to reshape his face like clay. Hopelessly addicted, Hagen was caught stealing more cream, and Daggett forced him to consume an entire barrel as punishment. However, instead of killing Hagen, the large dose turned him into a monster with only one thing on his muddy mind: revenge.

- As Clayface, Matt Hagen is no longer human. His entire body is made of muddy clay, which grants him shapeshifting abilities as well as super-strength.

- Clayface's power is limited only by his imagination. He can turn his limbs into lethal weapons by willing his muddy body into whatever shape he desires.

- Everything Clayface does revolves around his relentless pursuit of Roland Daggett, the man who made him into a freak. Clayface will do whatever it takes to get Daggett within his muddy grasp, regardless of who is hurt or killed in the process.

- Drawing upon his shapeshifting abilities and his experience as an actor, Clayface assumes the shapes and voices of others. These abilities make him a very difficult foe to detect.

BIOGRAPHIES

Laurie S. Sutton has read comics since she was a child. She grew up to become an editor for Marvel, DC Comics, Starblaze and Tekno Comics. She has written *Adam Strange* for DC, *Star Trek: Voyager* for Marvel, plus *Star Trek: Deep Space Nine* and *Witch Hunter* for Malibu Comics. There are long boxes of comics in her wardrobe where there should be clothing and shoes. Laurie has lived all over the world, and currently resides in Florida, USA.

Luciano Vecchio was born in 1982 and currently lives in Buenos Aires, Argentina. With experience in illustration, animation and comics, his works have been published in the US, Spain, UK, France and Argentina. His credits include *Ben 10* (DC Comics), *Cruel Thing* (Norma), *Unseen Tribe* (Zuda Comics) and *Sentinels* (Drumfish Productions).

GLOSSARY

antigravity reducing or cancelling out the effect of gravity

constrict squeeze

cryogenic chamber sealed room that freezes people's bodies when they die to preserve them

gravity force that pulls objects with mass together; gravity pulls objects down towards the centre of Earth

liquid nitrogen liquid formed after nitrogen gas is pressurized and cooled

prototype first version of an invention that tests an idea to see if it will work

radar device that uses radio waves to track the location of objects

sonar device that uses sound waves to find underwater objects; sonar stands for sound navigation and ranging

tendril long, thin, curling stem that helps plants attach to and climb up buildings

terabyte measure of large amounts of data; one thousand gigabytes

DISCUSSION QUESTIONS

1. Clayface stole prototype crime prevention technology and used it to commit crimes. Discuss two real-world technologies that could be used positively or negatively depending on who is using them.

2. Batman warns Robin that not all of the prototypes will work properly. Discuss a time when you built something that didn't work the way you had planned it to work.

3. Why did Batman and Robin use a cryogenic chamber to capture Clayface? Could they have stopped him another way? Explain your answers.

WRITING PROMPTS

1. Batman and Robin are known as the Dynamic Duo because they work as a team to capture super-villains. Write a short story about Batman and Robin where they use teamwork to capture a foe.

2. Clayface can change his body into any shape he chooses. If you could change shape, what shape would you morph into? Write about your new body shape, then draw it.

3. Batman and Robin use their acrobatic skills to battle Clayface in the antigravity sphere. Write a story about what it would be like to work in zero gravity as an astronaut on a space station.